THE MOST WONDERFUL GIFT in THE WORLD

Mark Sperring

Lucy Fleming

LITTLE TIGER
LONDON

It was Christmas morning and one last
present sat beneath the tree.
 "I bet it's mine!" giggled Esme.
 "No, mine!" whooped Bear.
But as they reached for the
red-wrapped gift, they noticed
something HUGELY surprising.
It wasn't for either one of them.
Not Esme . . . OR Bear!

The tag read *For Little Bunny Boo-Boo, Love Santa.*
"Well," said Esme, "in all the busy
JuMbLE - TuMbleNesS of Christmas, somebody's present
has been mixed up with ours."
BUT WHAT SHOULD THEY DO?

"Let's open it!" said Bear, giving it a BEARISH sniff.
Esme had a better idea. "Let's find Little Bunny Boo-Boo
and make sure she gets her gift!"

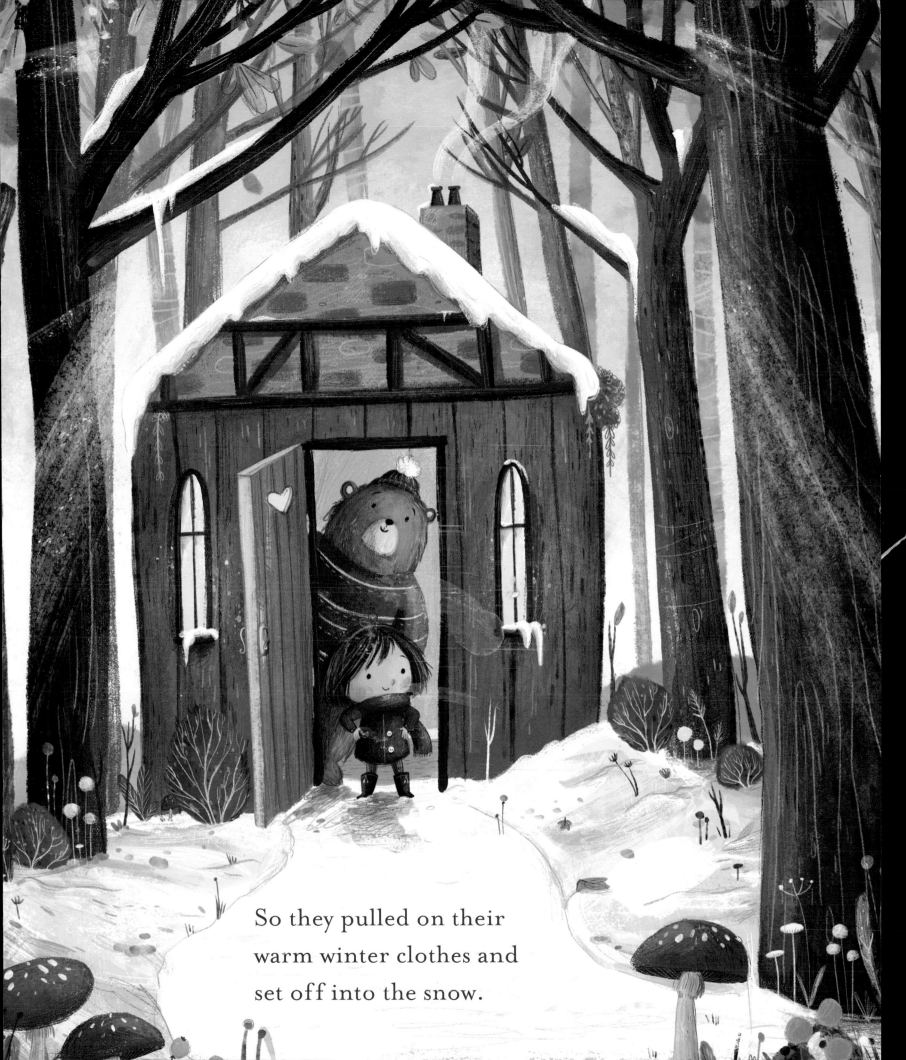

So they pulled on their
warm winter clothes and
set off into the snow.

They had not gone far when they came across a sign.

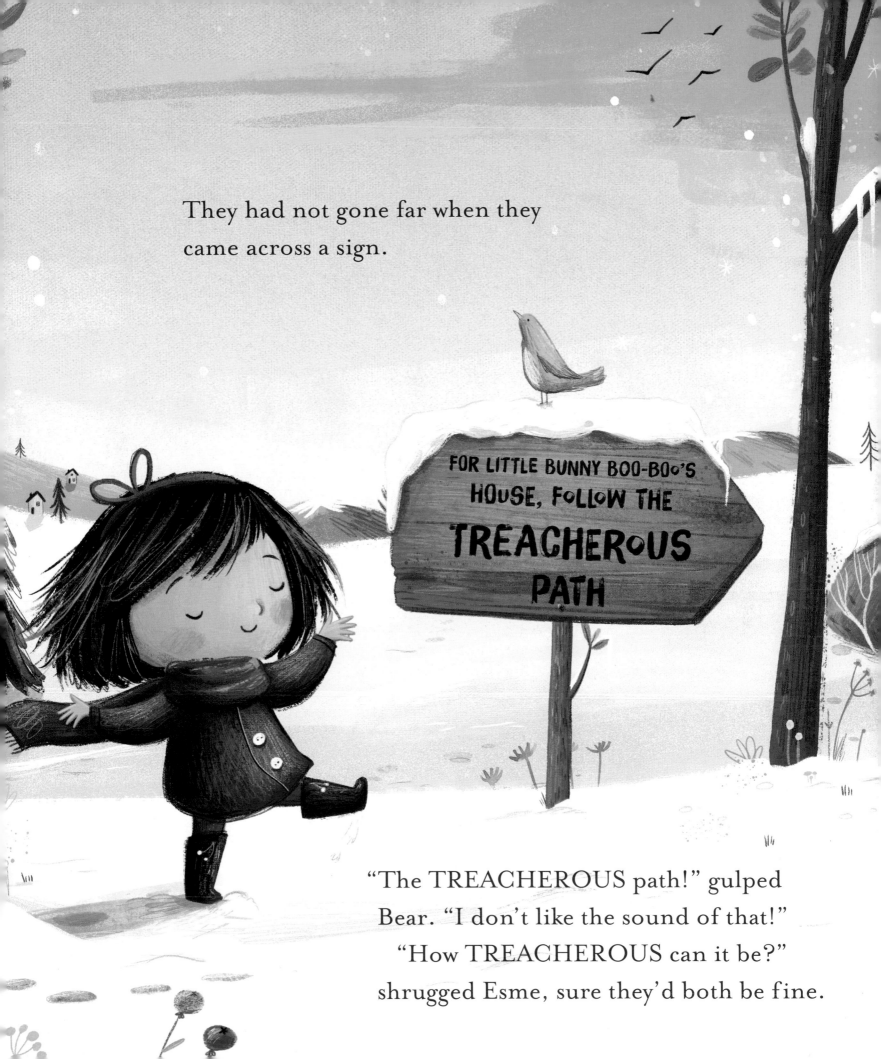

FOR LITTLE BUNNY BOO-BOO'S HOUSE, FOLLOW THE **TREACHEROUS PATH**

"The TREACHEROUS path!" gulped Bear. "I don't like the sound of that!"
"How TREACHEROUS can it be?" shrugged Esme, sure they'd both be fine.

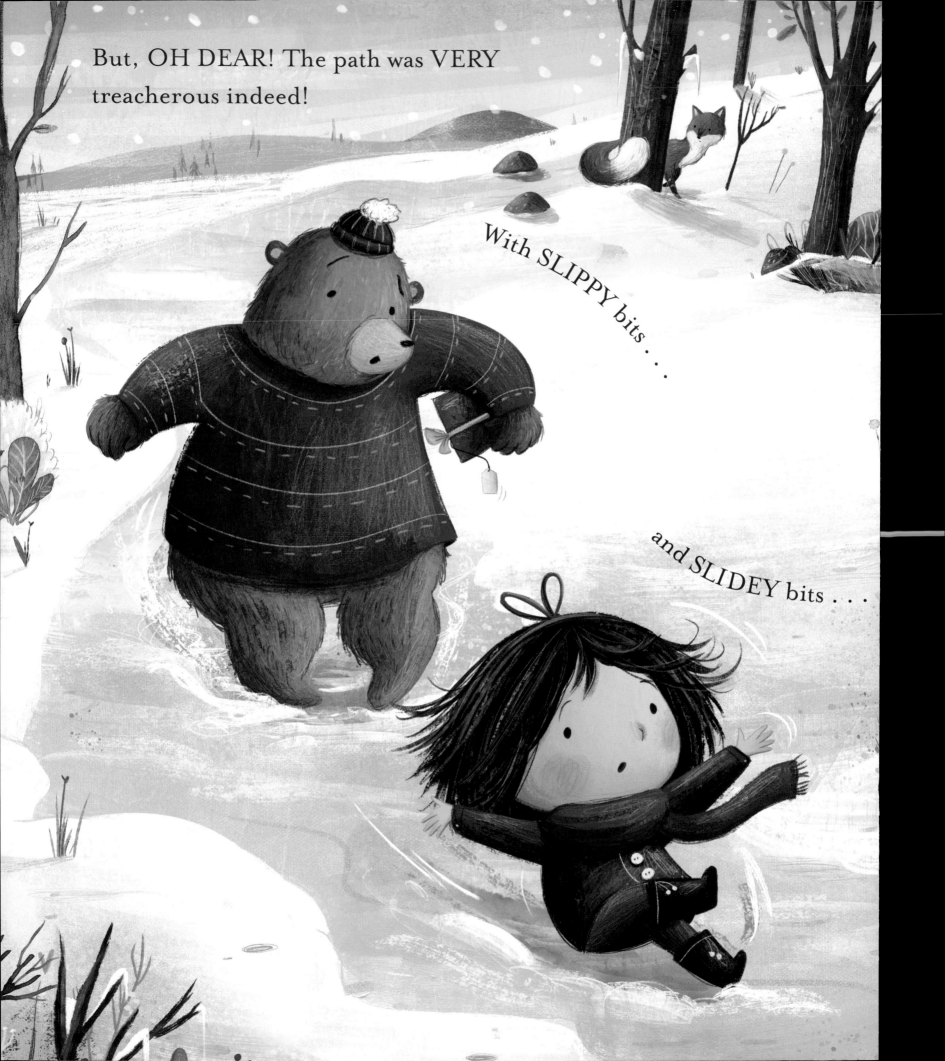

But, OH DEAR! The path was VERY treacherous indeed!

With SLIPPY bits . . .

and SLIDEY bits . . . .

and FALL-DOWN-ON-YOUR-BOTTOM bits!

BUMP!

After much slip-sliding about,
they came across another sign.

FOR LITTLE BUNNY BOO-BOO'S
HOUSE, WALK THROUGH THE
**HOWLING
GALE!**

Bear looked worried, but Esme gave him a comforting pat.

"How HOWLY can a gale be?" she said.

But suddenly the wind picked up and
blasted them full in the face . . .

Arooooooo

Arooooooooo!

"Can't we just keep Bunny Boo-Boo's present and go back home?" begged Bear.

"Of course not!" called Esme over the GROWLING-HOWLING GALE.

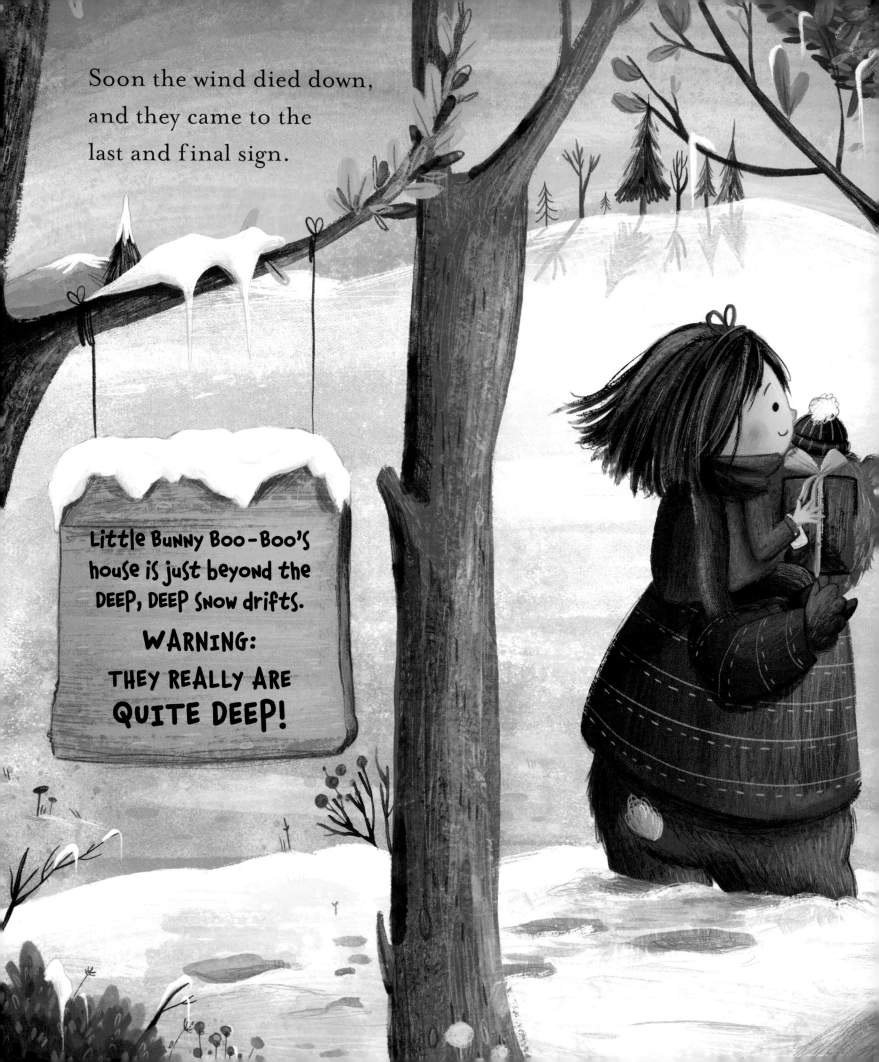

Soon the wind died down, and they came to the last and final sign.

Little Bunny Boo-Boo's house is just beyond the DEEP, DEEP snow drifts.
WARNING:
THEY REALLY ARE QUITE DEEP!

When the snow reached Esme's knees,
Bear scooped her high up onto his
shoulders and carried her, just like
that, for the rest of the way.

"Straight ahead for Bunny Boo-Boo's
house!" cheered Esme, as a twinkling
cabin came into view.

Well, when they reached the house,
they could not have been happier.
Firstly, Little Bunny Boo-Boo
seemed so pleased to see them.

Secondly, it was COSY-WARM!
And thirdly, when they looked around
they saw that Little Bunny Boo-Boo
had not received ONE SINGLE
Christmas present. Poor thing!

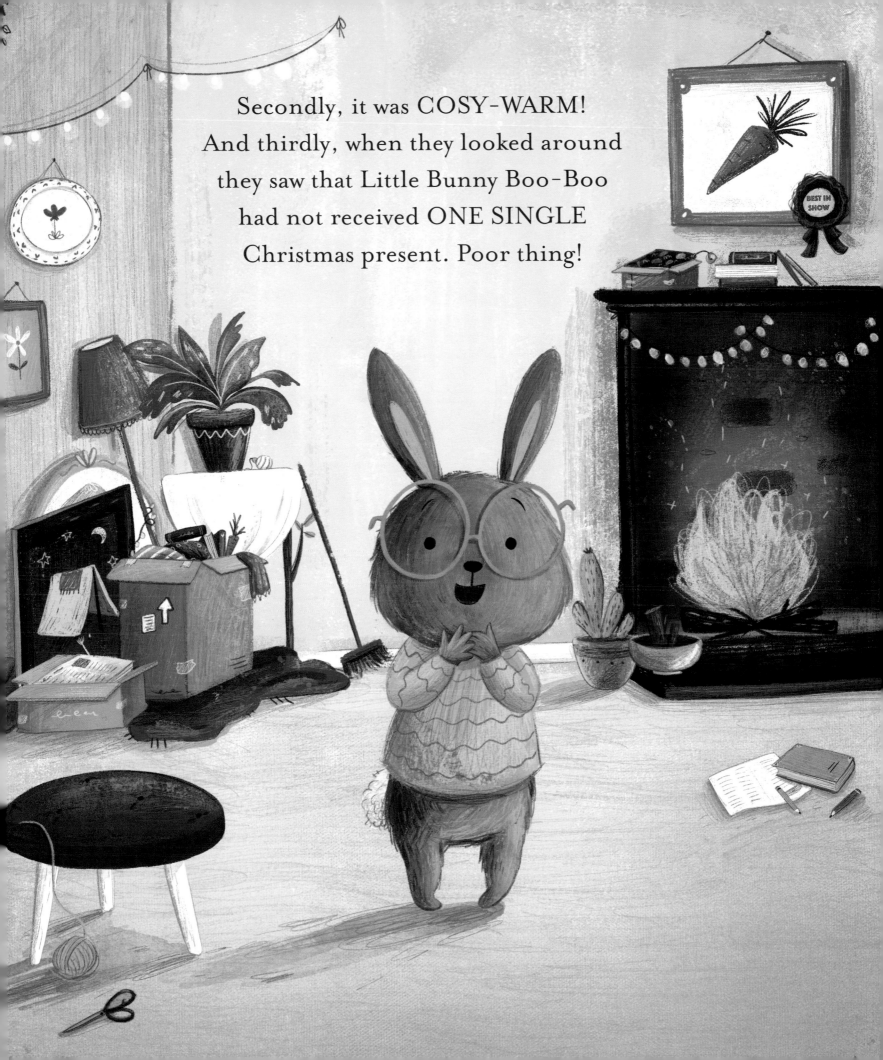

So Bear handed over the gift, and they all
huddled round to see what could be inside.
　"Maybe it's tiddlywinks!" smiled Esme.
　"Or peppermints!" beamed Bear.
　BUT imagine Esme and Bear's surprise when
Bunny Boo-Boo opened the gift and it was
ABSOLUTELY EMPTY with
NOTHING INSIDE AT ALL . . .

. . . except for a teeny-tiny handwritten note,
on the smallest scrap of paper.

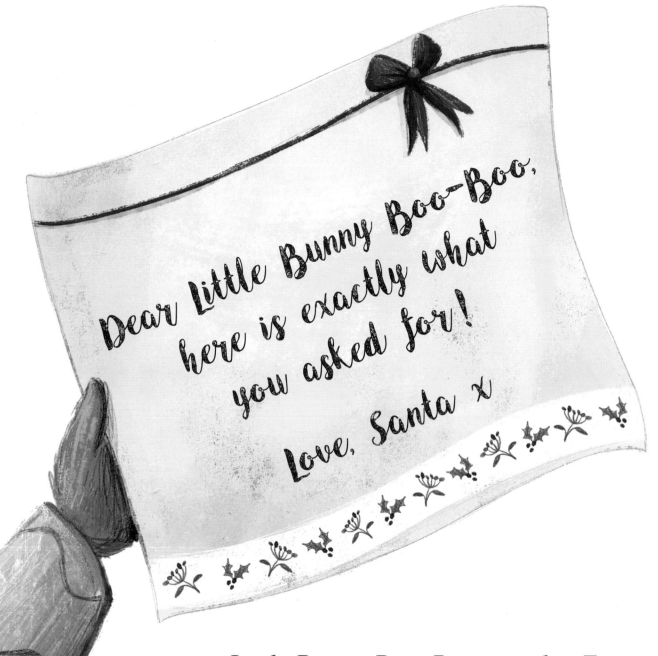

Dear Little Bunny Boo-Boo,
here is exactly what
you asked for!

Love, Santa x

Little Bunny Boo-Boo stared at Esme and
Bear and her eyes grew wide with joy.
"I've just moved into my little cabin," she said,
"and I haven't had time to make a single friend.
So, this year, I asked Santa for a VERY special gift . . ."

"A friend (perhaps even two) who was honest and true, who would walk a TREACHEROUS PATH, battle the HOWLIEST of GALES, and brave the DEEPEST OF SNOW DRIFTS just to stand by my side."

'So you see!" smiled Bunny Boo-Boo,
'Santa's present to me . . . IS YOU!"
"US?" said Esme and Bear,
thinking that perhaps a skipping
rope or spinning top might have
been better!

But after they'd enjoyed a Christmas Day
full of laughter and lovely things to eat, they
all agreed that things like skipping ropes
and spinning tops were very nice but . . .
a TRUE friend (perhaps even two) was the
BEST and MOST WONDERFUL gift of all!